DARK VOW

A COLLECTION OF MONSTROUS ROMANCE

KAYLA ST. JAMES

KRATERRA
ORC TERRITORY
HAIYA
THE CITADEL

BAERVAL ICEFIELDS

BAERVAL

NNELIN

KRATERRAN SEA

SALTWOOD FORTRESS

ASTES

IREDALE

Kraterran Kingdoms

KAYLA ST. JAMES

A DARK VOW

A COLLECTION OF MONSTEROUS ROMANCE

DARK VOW

The temple, surrounded by lush greenery, was like a peaceful oasis in the middle of a chaotic world. The early evening sunlight filtered through the trees, and created a kaleidoscope of colors and shadows on the grounds. The warmth of the sun on my shoulders was comforting, and the gentle melody of a nearby stream accompanied my steps as I walked toward the temple.

As the sun began to dip below the horizon it covered the forest in an orange-golden light that glowed off the temple stones. I felt the energy of the Maiden's love all around me and I leaned against the sun-warmed stone and admired the beauty of the goddess' secret sanctuary.

I took a deep breath and reaffirmed my connection to the goddess who dwelled in this place, and swore to protect it with all my heart and soul. This was a sacred place, and it filled me with peace and contentment more than any other place in all this world. I was honored to serve the Faceless Maiden in any way I could.

Crossing through the massive gates of the temple, I felt an

overwhelming sense of anticipation as I prepared myself to worship at her feet. Her spiritual presence seemed to permeate every inch of space around me and it filled me with longing as I moved around the temple walls to light the torches that had been set into the niches in the ancient stone.

Thousands of priestesses had walked this same path in the same pattern as I did. Thousands of priestesses had welcomed the prayers and worship of those who crossed through the Maiden's stone gates.

We were the conduit for their worship—through us, through our bodies, they would gain the Maiden's favor.

My instructions were clear, as always. When night fell, I would welcome the worshippers who had come to the temple.

As I stood in front of the Goddess' statue, I removed the silverblue pin that held my robe in place at my shoulder and let the dark fabric slide down my body. It fell at my feet in a soft cloud of dark blue watersilk and I pushed the silver pin into my hair as I stepped away from it.

I was completely naked, and the cool night air against my skin made me shiver. The priestesses of the Maiden's temple wore simple blue robes until the sun set, but from the moment the sun set, we were the tools of the goddess.

The slender band of silverblue that adorned my hair glinted in the torchlight. The gentle rustling of the breeze through the trees and the steady drip of the nearby fountain played in the background as I stood alone, my thoughts and feelings quieted, in the presence of the goddess.

Over the years I had lost count of how many pilgrims I had welcomed to her temple, how many had fallen to their knees before me and begged for her favor.

Each had their own desires, their own needs. I thought

about my own desires and needs for the first time that night, and my heart ached.

With a smile on my face, I walked through the temple to the sacred pool that graced the entrance to the temple.

I would begin my vigil there.

As I stepped into the water, my thoughts drifted to the first pilgrim I had ever welcomed to the temple—the very first that I had brought to the goddess.

I sank down in the water and closed my eyes as the sun-warmed water lapped over my naked skin.

My hands slipped down over my body as I basked in the goddess' presence and let the memory overtake me.

He'd been a hunter, my first, lost in the woods.

It had been a night much like this one. The pale light of the rising moon had painted the temple courtyard in a silvered glow, and I'd been waiting in the pool.

I was still new to the Goddess' call, but I'd known that he was coming.

I'd sensed his presence from the nearby woods, and I could feel the goddess' approval of what I was about to do.

The hunter had approached the pool with a frown upon his face—he was young and strong, powerfully built with large hands that were accustomed to holding weapons.

I smiled at him as I swam to the edge of the pool.

"Welcome, traveler," I said.

"What is this place?"

I rose up in the water, and felt a twinge in my belly as he watched the water roll off my breasts.

"You have found the Maiden's temple," I replied and extended a hand toward him. "You are welcome here."

He glanced back at the torchlit temple and then looked at me again, a frown on his ruggedly handsome face. The elegant point of his ears, marked with the notches of manhood rituals brought a new interest for me.

I'd never lain with an elf before...

He stepped closer, pulled by the power of the goddess, but his expression was still one of wary curiosity.

I could feel his desire—one that was more a healthy interest than an effect of the goddess' power.

"I've heard of this place," he said. "That the priestesses engage in—"

My smile did not fade as he approached. "It's true," I said. "Whatever you have heard is true."

I knew what people in the towns and villages said about us. That the temple was just a whorehouse in the forest. But they were wrong.

We took no coin in exchange for the favors of the goddess.

There was nothing sordid or clandestine about our worship.

"You look tired," I said. "Have you been walking long?"

He nodded. "I lost my companion just before sundown— We were in pursuit of a roebuck—"

I walked toward the edge of the pool and climbed the steps slowly. Bathed in moonlight, the water droplets that clung to my skin shimmered like precious gems and his mouth dropped open just a little as I came to stand before him.

"Come into the pool," I said. "Let the goddess wash away your fatigue."

He stood still as I loosened his belt and let it fall into the grass. He could have resisted any time, but he looked up at the stars as I pulled his tunic up over his head and dropped it to the ground beside his belt.

His chest and shoulders were thickly muscled and I rubbed my hands over his torso with breathless anticipation. The red-gold hair that covered his chest was soft under my palms and he let out a grunt as my hands fell to his hips and the edge of his breeches.

"I can do that," he murmured.

I bit my lip as my pussy throbbed. I could feel the pull of the goddess' power, and I was excited to perform my duties to her...excited for what lay ahead.

He unbuttoned his breeches and kicked off his boots with practiced motions and my breath caught as he pushed the leather down over his hips to reveal his cock.

I was certainly not innocent to the ways of carnal pleasure, but the sight of his member, thick and heavy against his thigh, filled me with a desire that was half selfish need, and half breathless anticipation for what was to come.

His cock pulsed as I stared, hardening as I watched and I smiled as I looked up into his pale eyes.

I took his hand and stepped closer so that I could press my naked body against his.

"Will you come into the pool?" I asked. "Will you worship the goddess with me?"

It was a line I had practiced many times until the High Priestess was satisfied, but it felt different to say it aloud in the darkness with the temple at my back and a hot body pressed against mine.

"I will," he replied. His voice was choked, but deep and strong, and a shiver rippled up my spine as I led him back to the pool.

I sank down into the water again and I could feel his eyes on me as he watched my naked body as it disappeared into the water.

He followed me into the water until it enveloped us up to our chins. The cool water against my skin was a relief and I closed my eyes briefly as it enveloped me—the embrace of the goddess.

I moved closer to him and the soft light from the torch on the temple steps caught his eyes and I could see the hesitation in his gaze.

There was a hunger there, but there was a fear there as well.

It was likely that he had heard more than just rumors of the pleasures of the temple. There were those who would spread terrible lies about the worship that went on here... I would have to do my best to quench his fears, as well as his lust.

I moved close to him, so close that my breasts brushed against his chest, my nipples tight with the chill of the water and anticipation.

"What is your name?" he asked. His voice was a whisper that trembled with desire.

I felt the thrum of the goddess' approval in my veins as I smiled.

"Erren," I replied. "But here, I am the only goddess."

I pressed my lips against his, and reveled in the scrape of his beard against my skin.

My nipples rubbed against his chest as I put my arms around his neck. My pussy was against his thigh, and I could feel the heat radiating off of him.

A shudder ran through his body as I reached down to touch him. I stroked him under the water, feeling the smoothness of the head of his cock and the rigid hardness of his cock. Silk over stone against my palm.

I broke the kiss and lifted my chin, pressing my lips to the curve of his neck, sucking and nibbling his skin.

He groaned, gripped my ass with his hands and lifted me up in the water. I wrapped my legs tight around him and I captured his mouth with mine.

A groan escaped him as his cock pressed against my entrance and I felt the heat rising from him. My breasts were pushed against his chest, goosebumps rippled across my skin where the cool night air touched me.

I clung to his shoulders, and as our tongues tangled together he lowered me onto him, filling me with his cock. I moaned into his mouth, overcome by the pleasure of his cock inside me.

The love of the goddess and her approval of the coupling flooded through me, bringing a new heat, and a different tightness into my belly.

His hands closed on my hips and he thrust into me. The water churned around us and lapped at the smooth stones at the edge of the pool as his cock slid deep inside me.

He fucked me hard and fast, his body gripping mine as he moved me through the water. Sweat broke out on my forehead, and I clung to him as he took me. He was stronger than any man I had ever been with, his hips pumping into mine, his cock filling me over and over again.

I sucked his bottom lip into my mouth and bit down with just enough pressure to make him groan. He drove forward, deep inside me, as I cried out. My orgasm ripped through me, and my pussy clenched around his huge cock.

My nails dug into the broad muscles of his shoulders as I urged him forward with my heels against his back.

His hips moved as he thrust into me with quick, animal motions, and I moaned with pleasure, clinging to him tighter.

I could feel the warmth rising in my belly, the tightness and pressure of the goddess' blessing. An orgasm swept over me, hard and fast and I cried out, the sound muffled by the water and his kiss.

The hot throb of his cock inside me was like a drumbeat, and his desire moved through me like a hot, molten river. My pussy clenched hard around his cock, milking him as he fucked me.

He thrust into me a few more times, hard and fast, and then he shuddered and groaned as his cock twitched and he emptied himself into me.

The warm gush of his seed inside me brought a new pulse of pleasure and I moaned into his mouth. Pleasure rippled through me, and the glow of the goddess' approval filled me.

He held me close, his hands still gripping my hips, until his hips slowed and the last waves of pleasure rocked our bodies.

I smiled, breathing hard, and kissed him again. He released me and pulled his cock from my aching pussy. I felt the emptiness at my core, but I did not doubt that the goddess was pleased with me, and my work was done.

I sank back into the water, exhausted, and then laughed as the hunter dunked himself into the pool, the water covering his head for a moment before he burst through the surface and rubbed his hands through his red-gold hair.

He kept his eyes on me as he climbed out of the pool and picked up his clothes.

"Come back tomorrow," I said softly. "As long as the goddess wants, I am yours."

He nodded, his eyes on me, and gathered his clothes and disappeared into the darkness. I closed my eyes and focused on the reverberations of the goddess' favor as they rumbled through my sated body.

The release was worship.

"As it shall be done," I murmured into the darkness. I had serviced many worshippers in, and alongside, this sacred pool. Even on the stones of the temple floor.

Humans from the Southlands, elves from the Midlands, traders from the icy wastes of the northern territories, and even orcs and werebeasts—all were welcome in the light of the goddess' sanctuary. If it was her favor they sought, it was mine to bestow without question.

The memories were deep and lingering, and my nipples were hard as I slid my fingers over them to tease and pluck at the already aching buds.

With one hand between my thighs, I arched against the pressure of my own palm, remembering another night in the service of the goddess.

Orcs were not common in these lands, the other priestesses spoke of them in awe and with an edge of fear in their voices... Weapons were not allowed within the temple's sacred confines, but that did not mean we were safe. There was a reason why I'd been given the long silverblue pin that I kept tucked into my robes or hidden in my hair.

For emergencies.

Something I hoped that I would never have to use.

But there was only one night that I'd worried that I would have to.

I'd only just finished lighting the torches when I heard their approach.

Heavy footsteps. The sound of heavy horses as they broke through the underbrush. *Warriors.*

I came to the edge of the temple stones and stared out into the gathering darkness.

"You are welcome here," I called out. "The Faceless Maiden turns away no one who would come to her temple to worship."

There was a grunt from the forest, and I forced myself to smile. I could not let them, whoever they were, know that I was nervous. I was not a victim. I was not a sacrifice.

I was the goddess' chosen vessel.

That was all the power I needed.

Two hulking shapes materialized between the trees and my breath caught.

"If you would come to worship at the goddess' feet, you must leave your weapons with your horses."

My voice echoed in the darkness, and my words were answered with a dark chuckle.

"Bold words, Priestess."

"It is our custom here," I called out. "This temple is dedicated to the Faceless Maiden, and the pursuit of her greatest gifts. A temple of love and the worship of its many forms. If you mean ill will here, then I will ask you to pass by."

"And if we do not pass?"

I swallowed hard as one of the large silhouettes stepped into the torchlight.

An orc.

He was unbelievably tall and thickly muscled. Dark war braids hung with gold rings fell over his shoulders. His deep green skin was mottled with scars, and his tusks were banded with thick rings of silverblue that glittered in the torchlight.

I straightened my shoulders and did not look away. I could not show weakness. Not now.

"And how would you defend yourself, Priestess," the orc called out, "if we meant you harm?"

His voice was full of menace, but I could sense some teasing in his tone. This was a test of my faith, and my trust in the goddess. And I could not deny the twinge of lust that rippled through my body as I looked the warrior up and down.

A powerful specimen.

And then the second orc stepped into the light. Just as tall and broad as his companion, this orc's head was shaved of its braids, and was instead covered in intricate tattoos in black ink.

His tusks were pierced with silverblue rings, and his pale eyes burned into mine.

I spread my arms wide. "And why would you wish me harm?" I asked. "You have heard the stories of this temple, have you not?"

The first orc nodded.

"Isn't that why you're here?"

They approached the temple slowly and my smile did not falter. They were not carrying any weapons. They were testing me, as was the goddess. I could bear this test.

"The stories of the Faceless Maiden, and the impassioned pursuits of those who worship her, are not false. They are true. If you are seeking the object of your desire, in the pursuit of passion and devotion, then you have come to the right place."

There was a moment of silence as the two orcs exchanged a look. Then the taller one let out a deep guttural laugh and nodded.

"Very well, Priestess," he said, his voice rumbling like thunder in the darkness. "We will accept your terms."

I turned and walked back toward the temple, and then stopped as the two orcs exchanged another look.

"Have you no questions?"I asked. "No concerns about our customs here?"

I heard a low laugh from behind me and the sound of footsteps.

"Our only concern, Priestess," the first orc said as he stepped up behind me and wrapped his enormous hand around my waist, "is how quickly we can worship the goddess."

I shivered as the orc behind me tightened his grip, the sensation of his iron-hard hand against my body sent a shock of pleasure through me.

The tattooed orc circled in front of me and I trembled as he ran his thick fingers through my hair and pulled my head back to expose my throat.

"Speak only if you're spoken to," he murmured.

I nodded, my body shaking as the orc behind me pressed against me, his thick cock hard against my ass. I turned my head to look at the orc behind me. His skin was faintly reflecting the torchlight and I could see the glint of something in his eyes.

Hunger. Power.

And the desire to dominate a priestess.

"I am your vessel, Goddess," I whispered softly, the words slipping out of my mouth before I could hold them back.

"They didn't tell us how beautiful she would be," the tattooed orc growled.

I shivered as his hands slid down over my body, teasing me, promising me pleasure and pain at the same time. I craved both.

"I trust that the first to worship in this temple will not be disappointed," I said, knowing who that first worshiper would be.

The orc who held my hips pressed his body close behind me, his strong hands palming my breasts and my ass roughly. I gasped as his massive cock pressed against my back, and his teeth raked across my shoulder.

The tattooed orc's hands slid over my hips and down to cup my ass, and the other one growled.

"I would like to be first," the tattooed orc said, his voice low and husky. "The first to bask in the temple's firelight. I would like to be the first to worship here tonight."

I reached for the silverblue pin that held my dark blue robes in place and tugged it free.

The silken fabric slithered down my body and I smiled as the expression in the orc's pale eyes changed. Lust battling with whatever else he might have had planned.

"And you shall be," I said.

"We'll both worship in this temple tonight," the orc behind me said suddenly. He pulled my hair back and hissed, "Will you welcome two orcs into your temple, Priestess? Will you service us as your Goddess commands?"

I felt the length of his steel-hard cock against my ass and I shivered with anticipation. I turned my head to look at him, and for a moment, I was startled by the look in the orc's eyes.

The same hunger that I recognized on the face of the tattooed orc was mirrored there.

"Of course," I whispered. "The goddess wishes it."

I moaned softly as the tattooed orc palmed my breasts, pinching the nipples to hardness with quick strokes that were equal amounts of pleasure and pain.

My pussy throbbed with need and my mouth watered to taste them.

The orc behind me groaned as his enormous hand dragged down over my hip and thrust between my thighs.

I moaned again and arched into his hand to rub my clit against his thick fingers. Begging him without words to give me what I wanted.

"Tell us how you would worship us, Priestess," the tattooed orc said as he grabbed hold of my throat and stepped closer still.

His hand was strangely gentle as it wrapped around my throat. He could have cut off my breath with the slightest movement, but he used only enough pressure to make me gasp with desire as my breath caught.

I was surrounded by their scent, and the heat that radiated between them.

"I would give myself to you," I whimpered as the orc behind me teased his thick fingers against my clit and then thrust them deep into my pussy. "I would give my body to you."

"As your goddess demands?" the tattooed orc asked.

"Yes," I moaned.

The tattooed orc released his hold on my throat and pushed his hand into my hair; his hand cupped the back of my head and held me as tight as his companion fucked my pussy with his thick fingers.

I looked up into his pale eyes and shivered.

"I would taste you," I whispered.

"Both of us," the orc behind me growled as his tusks brushed against my shoulder.

"Yes," the tattooed orc whispered, stepping closer still. "That's it. Show us how much you want us."

My breath caught in my throat as I looked up into his face. His eyes burned with lust and wrath, and he would not be denied. I could see it in his eyes, and I wanted him. I wanted both of them.

The orc behind me grabbed my arms and pulled them behind my back as the tattooed orc pulled me close and ran his tongue across my lips. The bearded orc behind me continued the furious motion of his hand, his thick fingers stretched my entrance and made me moan with lust and need.

"You are the priestess and we are the worshippers," he growled. "You will receive us as the goddess commands."

My pussy clenched in anticipation and I whimpered as I opened my mouth to him.

"Please," I whispered. "Please."

"Please *what*, Priestess?"

The tattooed orc's voice was rough as he grabbed my hips and thrust against me.

"Please take me."

The bearded orc's fingers withdrew from my aching pussy and I fell to my knees on the temple stones.

The orcs circled me, and I watched them hungrily, their thick cocks outlined against the leather of their breeches. The tattooed orc unlaced his breeches with practiced motions and I gasped aloud as his cock sprang free. It was pierced along the underside with three, thick silverblue rings that clicked as his cock pulsed.

The bearded orc dropped his breeches with equal speed, and I swallowed hard to see the thick length of his cock, standing proud and hard, pierced with two thick rings that gleamed in the torchlight.

I'd heard about the way orc's fucked... and I thought I was ready... but two of them?

The orc warriors circled me, their cockheads were hard and wet with their pre-cum, and I was desperate to taste it.

"To the Goddess," I murmured. "I submit."

The orcs growled as I leaned my head back and reached up to wrap my hands around each of their cocks. I stroked them gently at first, teasing my thumbs over the thick rings and coaxed groans from their throats as I did so.

Feeling bold, I pumped my hands up and down the lengths of the powerful orc cocks. I loved the way they throbbed in my hands, the way they grew harder and harder with every stroke.

I loved the way the rings caught the torchlight and gleamed.

I loved the way their eyes burned with lust.

I licked my lips and pulled the tattooed orc's cock toward my lips. My mouth watered for the taste of him. I traced my tongue over the head of his cock, catching the droplets of pre-cum as they appeared and then sucked the head of the cock into my mouth.

The orc moaned as I swirled my tongue around the head, tasting it.

The taste of him was heady. Like a drug. My pussy throbbed in time with my heartbeat.

I stroked the bearded orc's cock faster, and felt my pussy

grow even wetter at the sounds of pleasure I was drawing from them. The orcs groaned and the bearded orc reached down to grip my breasts hard, squeezing and pulling my nipples, hard enough to make me moan again.

The tattooed orc grabbed my hair and pulled my head back. I opened my mouth wider as his cock slid across my tongue and I teased my fingers across the thick rings of his piercings.

Their cocks were the same length, although the tattooed orc's was slightly thicker. The rings heavier and more finely crafted.

I moaned, my entire body thrumming with arousal. My pussy clenched in anticipation, and my mouth watered for more.

"All of it," the tattooed orc growled. "Take them both into your mouth."

I sucked the tattooed orc's cock deep into my mouth and rubbed my tongue over the silverblue rings to make him groan. The tattooed orc tightened his grip in my hair and fucked my mouth. He thrust into me, slow and deep, and then pulled almost all the way out, so that I could take a ragged breath.

The bearded orc thrust his cock into my hand, and I drew it to my mouth, hungry to taste him and do as I'd been commanded.

He didn't wait for me to tease him, and he thrust hard into my mouth. I moaned around his hard length as his cockhead brushed against the back of my throat, and I sucked my cheeks in as he did so, my tongue rubbing against the silverblue rings that pierced the underside of his cock as he slid out.

The tattooed orc pushed his companion aside. I

swallowed hard and my pussy clenched. I looked up into the tattooed orc's pale eyes, parted my lips, and moaned as he slid his cock deep into my mouth.

I loved the way the veins pulsed against my tongue, the way his cock felt as it slid deeper into my mouth. I swallowed and squeezed my eyes closed as the tattooed orc groaned and his grip on my hair tightened.

I sucked and teased the thick head, pulling my lips back and then sliding them forward again. My tongue flicked against the underside of his cock, teasing against the silverblue rings as it slid deep into my throat again and again.

The tattooed orc groaned aloud.

With a frustrated growl, the bearded orc pulled his cock from my hand and moved behind me. I moaned as a thick finger slid deep into my pussy.

I pushed my hips back to meet it, and spread my knees wider to let him in as the tattooed orc thrust deeper into my throat.

The bearded orc's fingers were rough as he thrust them inside of me, and I whimpered.

They were rough and hard, but I wanted them.

I wanted them to use me.

The tattooed orc pulled his cock from my mouth with a groan as the bearded orc behind me pushed me onto my hands and knees.

One enormous hand slid over my ass while the other pumped his thick fingers in and out of my pussy. "Is this what you want, priestess," he growled throatily. "Is this what you want?"

I moaned, my entire body thrumming with arousal as I looked back at him over my shoulder.

"Yes," I breathed. "Oh yes."

"You want more."

"Yes."

"You want us to fill you. You want us to fuck you. You want us to take you, together."

"Yes," I whispered. "My Goddess, yes."

The tattooed orc grabbed my hips and plunged his cock deep into my pussy as the tattooed orc pushed his cock into my mouth once more. My cries were choked and muffled by his cock. The feeling of the two cocks sliding into me like that, stretching me, made my skin tingle.

The bearded orc groaned as he slid his hands around to grab my breasts, and then leaned forward to pinch my nipples hard.

I yelped, but the cry ended in a strangled moan as the tattooed orc's fingers slid into my mouth to feel his own cock as I sucked it.

Tears streamed down my cheeks and I whimpered with need, as the bearded orc growled, pulled me back toward him and slammed into me.

The two orcs thrust into me together, deeper and harder. The bearded orc's cock fucked my pussy, and my whole body shuddered as the thick rings of his piercings rubbed deep inside me. I cried out around the tattooed orc's thick cock and I sucked him deep into my throat.

The orcs groaned as they slammed into me, their cocks pounding into me from both sides as I moaned and sobbed and begged for more.

"Please," I whispered. "Please."

The tattooed orc slid his cock from my mouth and grabbed my hair once more. "Beg us," he whispered. "Beg us to fuck you."

"Please," I gasped. "Please fuck me. Please fill me."

The tattooed orc's cock was slick with my saliva as he pulled me forward. My knees scraped across the temple stones as he laid on his back and pulled me over him.

An angry roar filled the air as the bearded orc's cock pulled free of my pussy, and I groaned at the loss of fullness and stretch that I craved.

I panted with need as the tattooed orc positioned the head of his thick cock at my eager entrance.

I could see the forest, the shadowed moonlight, the stars above... but my vision was blurred with lust and the edge of the orgasm I'd sought so diligently was just beyond my reach.

Thick, strong hands grabbed my hips as the bearded orc yanked me back and caused the head of the tattooed orc's cock to slide deep into my pussy. I gasped as the fullness took me by surprise.

The bearded orc spread my ass and pushed his cockhead against my asshole.

I whimpered.

"Please," I begged. "Please, I need this."

His cock slid into my ass slowly, and I felt the thick silverblue rings of his piercings slide inside of me. I shivered as I felt them slide against my walls, as the feeling of being full of cock grew and spread through my body.

The tattooed orc groaned as my pussy spasmed around him, and my back arched as the bearded orc's cock slid deeper into my ass.

"Please," I begged. "Please, please, please."

I gasped as the orc's massive cock drove deep into my ass until he was buried to the hilt inside me.

The stones bit into my knees and my fingers grasped the cold stone as the orc gripped my hips and fucked me from behind.

His every thrust sent another wave of pleasure through my body. He was so deep inside me, ravaging me, plunging into an orifice that had never been filled before. And yet, I wanted more.

I wanted it all.

The tattooed orc shifted under me, and I could feel the thick silverblue rings dragging over the most sensitive parts of my body.

The feeling of him in me, combined with the thick rings that pierced their cocks sent delicious thrills of sensation through my body, was almost too much.

I was so close. The goddess was so near.

"Please," I begged. "Please, please. Please."

The tattooed orc grabbed my hips and pulled me down on him as he thrust deep inside of me. The bearded orc grunted and did the same, fucking my ass with renewed vigor, stretching me and holding me open as they used my body.

The rings on that tattooed orc's cock pulled and scraped as he slid inside my pussy, and the feeling of the hard flesh of his cock dragging against my inner walls was too much.

"Do it," the tattooed orc growled. "Do it! Cum on my cock, Priestess!"

"Cum on my cock," the bearded orc groaned. "My hard cock in your ass!"

My back arched as the orgasm washed over me. My whole body jerked and shuddered as I came—hard.

Wave after wave of pleasure broke over me, and I lost myself in the moment.

The orgasm was so intense and the moment so perfect that the only thing that mattered to me was the pleasure.

All I knew was how good it felt to be with two massive,

powerful orc warriors. To be filled with their thick cocks, and to be taken so hard and so completely.

Below me, the tattooed orc's eyes closed and he groaned as his cock swelled inside me.

My whole body tightened. I moaned louder, louder, louder. Rode him harder, opened myself more to the cock in my ass. Sensed their orgasm growing closer and closer.

The air was thick and hot with the scent of sex as the orcs fucked me hard and fast. Beneath me, the tattooed orc groaned as his cock swelled and twitched deep in my pussy.

"Goddess," the bearded orc growled and thrust into me.

"Yes," I cried out, "Yes, yes. Fill me."

He thrust, once, twice, and I felt his cock twitch inside of me.

I moaned as the bearded orc's cock swelled in my ass, unbearably large and hard.

With roars that echoed in the darkness, the orcs came almost in unison. Powerful jets of hot cum filled my ass and then my pussy. Breeding both my holes.

The orgasm that broke over me was unlike any I'd had before. Two monstrous men, each filling me with their seed.

The pleasure was so intense, so powerful that it was almost painful, and yet I wanted more.

I wanted it to go on forever.

I felt like I was going to fly apart, that my body couldn't hold back so much pleasure, but I didn't care. I embraced it, savored it, and it was perfect.

I collapsed onto the tattooed orc's chest, the leather straps of his harness bit into my cheek, but I didn't care.

I moaned aloud as they reluctantly withdrew their cocks from my body and I felt the heat of their cum as it trickled out of my pussy and my ass and smeared over my thighs.

My legs shook, and my body was so weak from the experience I could barely keep myself upright.

My pussy was sore, my asshole was sore, and yet all I wanted was more.

I didn't know how much I would be able to handle, but my body craved more and my blood sang with the goddess' approval.

"Take me to the pool," I murmured.

With a grunt, the tattooed orc, sat up and gathered me in his powerful arms. I couldn't have weighed more than a feather to him as he stood and strode from the temple toward the sacred pool that lay just beyond the gatestones.

"Is your goddess pleased?" the orc asked as he stepped down into the pool.

I sighed as the water lapped over my ankles and then my knees as he waded deeper.

"She is," I said with a smile. "Your worship has been accepted and the Faceless Maiden's blessings will follow you on your journey."

I could tell that the tattooed orc was surprised and pleased by the news, but he only grunted as he lowered me down into the pool.

"We ride south," he said. "Are there other places we might worship—"

"Of course," I said. "You will find the Faceless Maiden's worship in all corners of the Empire. You will be welcomed there."

He nodded and then waded out of the pool. My aching pussy clenched as I watched the water stream off his muscled ass and down his powerful thighs.

Orcs were terrifying in their beauty, and I could say that for certain now.

The bearded orc had pulled on his breeches once more, and he regarded me carefully from the edge of the pool as his companion stepped into his breeches.

They said nothing more before they turned toward the dark woods and disappeared from sight.

My head fell back against the soft moss at the side of the pool and I let out a satisfied sigh as I stared up at the stars that wheeled overhead.

"Your will be done, Goddess," I murmured and then I gasped as a familiar sensation burned its way across my skin.

The marks of the goddess' favor.

I had many of them now.

Two intricate runes, dark against my burnished skin, the same ones that appeared after each of my encounters, etched their way onto my chest just below my collarbones.

I bit my lip to keep from crying out as the burning of the marks intensified and then faded. Pain and pleasure at the same time.

"Thank you," I whispered.

I ducked down into the pool and let the cool water cover my head. I felt closest to the goddess here, and I imagined that I could hear her voice as she sang to me.

The other priestesses must have thought I was strange—but my sisters whispered behind my back for other reasons, too. Tonight's ceremony would be talked about for months to come.

I regretted nothing. This calling was not one for those who would regret.

The orcs had left, and I found that I was strangely saddened by their absence. My body ached in places I hadn't thought possible before, but I felt glorious.

. . .

It had been years ago since my first orc warriors had entered the temple... but I remembered the feel of them well. The thickness of their cocks, the powerful grip of their hands on my body as they'd used me—as the goddess had used me.

Transcendent.

The pool water shimmered in the moonlight as my hand worked between my thighs, teasing my clit with gentle strokes. I wasn't seeking immediate release, but a gentle build of erotic pleasure, my own form of worship in the goddess' presence.

This was how I began every evening in the goddess' service.

Alone, in the sacred pool I would let my memories become my worship.

My skin was marked with hundreds of intricate runes now, and I remembered each encounter. Each worshiper.

Tentative, commanding, innocent... all seeking the same thing. Release. Domination. Submission. Penance. I gave each of them what they needed. That was my calling. That was how I showed my devotion to the Faceless Maiden.

A flare of desire raced through my body as my fingers moved through my slick folds.

I remembered the way the bearded orc had thrust into my ass, stretching me more than I thought I could bear. The tattooed orc had felt just as thick when he'd filled me to bursting with his cock.

My nipples puckered as I ducked low in the water and held them just above the surface. The coldness of the water against my skin made the pleasure of my touch even sharper.

The memory of the tattooed orc's hard cock as it pistoned in and out of my pussy made me moan aloud as my fingers worked my clit. I ached to feel that same fullness again.

I closed my eyes and imagined the muscular warriors with their long, thick cocks. I imagined fucking them, feeling the agonizing rub of the silverblue rings that pierced their cocks inside me, giving my body over to their every desire. Being their woman—their gift to the goddess.

I bit my lip as my climax built with a steady rhythm... but I wasn't ready to take my own pleasure. Not yet.

On another night as the temple's caretaker, I'd stayed awake almost until the first of Kraterra's moons had set below the horizon—hours before dawn. The torchlight flickered low and I could smell the arrival of a new day on the air. No one had come to the temple that night, but that was not a strange thing.

There were many nights that I had spent in silent, solitary reflection, and they were just as rewarding as the ones that commanded my service to the worshippers who came to stand before the Faceless Maiden.

I sighed with contentment as I laid in the grass beside the sacred pool and watched the stars wheel above me.

It had been a strange day. One of the sisters had been released from her vows—she had fallen in love with one of the worshippers and broken the goddess' commandments.

She had stood before her sisters, marked with the goddess runes, and had shed no tears as those marks were removed—carved from her flesh with bone handled knives wielded by silent priestesses. The wounds were slathered in a salve that would be certain to leave a scar when they healed... a purposeful choice. And one that would ensure that she would bear the marks of her betrayal for the rest of her life.

But she had stood there, proud and unwavering, the roundness of her pregnancy evident through the sheer material of her robes.

Robes that she was stripped of as the final mark was removed.

She was proud of her choice.

Her lover waited beyond the temple grounds, held back by priestesses who would not hesitate to cut his throat if necessary.

I'd watched it all with a kind of mute horror. I'd never wondered what it might be like to leave the goddess' service. I had never imagined that such a thing would happen to me.

I loved my duties here and on that particular night, I was even more determined to perform my sacred duties.

Disappointment flooded through me as the night wore on, but then I heard something strange on the wind.

Singing.

A melody unlike anything I'd ever heard before.

I sat up in the grass and my heart pounded in my chest as the melody flowed through my veins.

Beautiful.

Intoxicating.

My eyes drifted closed as the singer drew closer.

His voice was smooth and rich, the tone of it touching something deep within me that I hadn't known I possessed. The longing in his voice, the ache—I longed to give him what he desired, and hoped that it might be enough.

Before I knew what was happening, I was on my feet, pulled by his song toward the edge of the forest.

But at the last ring of torchlight, I felt suddenly cold.

"What—"

The singing had stopped, but I wasn't alone.

"You are welcome here," I called out. "The Faceless Maiden welcomes all who would approach her temple with love in their hearts..."

"Pretty words, Priestess," a voice replied from the darkness. "But does your goddess welcome *any* who would enter her domain?"

"Of course," I said. "No one has ever been turned away from these stones."

A thrill of desire prickled up my spine at the tone of his voice.

"Were you the one who was singing just now," I asked. "The song was—lovely."

"I thank you," the stranger replied, "my mother taught it to me when I was just a child."

As he stepped out of the trees and into the torchlight, my breath caught at his beauty. I had welcomed all kinds of worshippers to the goddess' temple. Men and women of all ages, all body shapes, and more races than I could count... but he surpassed them all.

Long white hair spilled over his shoulders like a waterfall, and his high cheekbones were sharp and pronounced, giving him an angular look that was at once strange and hauntingly beautiful.

His eyes... his eyes were black.

I swallowed hard as I stared at him.

His eyebrow rose slightly. "Am I welcome here, Priestess?"

Without hesitation, I extended my hand toward him. "Of course."

He set his hand upon mine and my breath caught as his fingers touched my palm.

The familiar thrill of the goddess' approval raced through my body.

"Where have you come from?" I asked.

His smile was unreadable.

"East," he said.

"What lies to the east?"

He looked at me strangely. "Do you not know what lies east of your holy temple?"

I shook my head. "I was born here."

"Really?"

"The priestesses bear children—true children of the goddess. We are taken into her service and then the fortunate few are chosen to act as her conduits... her vessels."

"Vessels?"

I nodded and gestured toward the temple. "We welcome any who would come to worship at the feet of the goddess. We worship with our minds, our bodies, our hearts, our intentions—"

"Intentions—"

"You have heard stories of this place," I said with a smile. "That we are no better than whores—"

"I have heard nothing," he chuckled.

"Be that as it may," I said. "It is not the case. Not every penitent is chosen by the goddess to receive her favors."

"And how are such decisions made?"

His black eyes captivated me and I bit down on my tongue to remind myself of my duties.

"The goddess speaks to us—in subtle ways—to let us know that she has granted her favor to a particular worshiper."

"Do you have a choice in the matter?"

I looked up at the stars and smiled. "Whatever the goddess chooses, it is my honor to fulfil her wishes."

"I see."

He stopped just at the edge of the temple stones and turned toward the sacred pool.

"Do you swim in the pool," he asked.

"I do," I replied. "I feel closest to the goddess when I am in her sacred waters. I can feel her voice there. Hear it—"

I didn't know why I was telling him such things, it felt wrong, but the pulse of the goddess' desire thrummed in my veins and she had not stopped me from sharing myself—something I never did with the worshippers who came to this temple.

To them, I was a nameless vessel—a conduit to the goddess. But this man... this man was different.

I thought of the young priestess who had forsaken her vows to be with her lover...

No.

"You did not tell me what is east of here," I said.

"Didn't I?"

"No."

He looked up at the stars and then back to me. His black eyes bored into mine, reflecting the glimmer of the stars and the glow of the torchlight. Ice and fire reflected in their dark depths.

Mesmerizing.

"The sea," he said. "A great inland sea of dark water, rough waves... salt spray..."

"I have never seen anything like that," I murmured. "Why did you leave it?"

His smile was bitter. "I was cast out by my people. Sent to wander..."

I laid a hand upon his cheek. "That was cruel of them."

He chuckled and turned his head to press his lips against my palm. "No one would agree with you."

I wanted to ask him why he had been cast out—but that was not my role. I had already said too much.

"I can give you comfort," I said. "The Maiden forgives all, and looks upon all those who would come before her with love with a favorable eye... Do you wish to continue your journey with her blessing?"

His smile was soft as he grasped my hand and pulled it away from his cheek.

"And you would give that to me? The blessing of a Faceless Goddess?"

I nodded and laid my other hand against his chest. "I would. She has already made her intentions known."

He was so close and I gripped the soft linen of his shirt to pull him closer.

His lips brushed against mine. "Are you a virgin?" he whispered.

I shook my head, the pressure building inside me hardened my nipples and made my pussy clench. "No."

"And those marks on your body. They're not just ritual tattoos."

"They're not tattoos," I replied. "They show the number of times I've given the goddess' blessing." His eyes widened. "It is a privilege to be chosen as the goddess' vessel," I whispered. "I have been with men and women, I can be whatever you need."

Without warning, he pressed his lips against mine again

and I moaned into his mouth as his hands dragged down my body.

I pulled the silver pin from the shoulder of my robes, and he groaned as the silken fabric slid down my body.

He unbuckled his belt and pulled his tunic over his head to reveal a lithe, angular torso, lightly muscled as though he had spent a lifetime swimming in the salt sea he had spoken of.

His hands were large and callused, but so gentle as he dragged them down my hips. My own hands were frantic with need as I pulled at the laces of his leather breeches.

His muscles flexed beneath my fingers as his breeches loosened and I slid them down his thighs.

His cock was long and thick, and saliva flooded my mouth as I looked at it. He shuddered as my fingertips grazed against his hipbone.

I stepped closer and smiled as he shuddered again. His hand rested on my hip, his grip like iron, and I felt a thrill run through me as I imagined what he could do to me with those hands.

I moved closer still and pressed my naked body against his so that I could feel his cock against my belly. It pulsed with the desire that I could feel flowing from him.

"You are welcome here," I murmured. "Beloved of the goddess, bask in her light."

My hand dragged down his thigh and he stiffened as my fingers brushed against his cock.

"If you do not wish for it—"

"I do," he choked out.

His cock throbbed under my hand and the desire that he was holding back pulsed against my palm. I stroked him until my hand was slick with the evidence of his desire. He groaned as I fell to my knees and took his smooth cock into my mouth.

I wanted to feel every inch of him, wanted to taste him, wanted to show him with my actions that I was there to obey his every command.

The heat of his cock was divine as it slid into my mouth, and the sound that came from him—half plea and half moan—filled me with a coiled desire that thrummed in the pit of my stomach.

I sucked him until my cheeks hollowed and my mouth ached and I could taste the saltiness of him as his lust leaked onto my tongue.

"I need to be inside you," he gasped out.

I slid my hands up his thighs and dug my nails into his flesh as he pulled his cock from my mouth.

He took hold of my arms and lifted me up to my feet. I wrapped my arms around his neck and bit back a gasp as he gripped my waist and lifted me higher.

Instinct guided me as I wrapped my legs around his hips

"I need you," he whispered.

"Then have me," I whispered back. "I am yours."

His cock pressed against my core, and I rubbed against it shamelessly, moaning as his cock throbbed against my clit.

As I wrapped my legs around his waist, he walked toward the sacred pool, my body tight against his muscular chest. I could feel his heart beating against mine, the pulse matched my own. Beat for beat.

He pressed his lips against my ear. "You are certain you want this," he whispered.

Drawing his earlobe between my teeth, I made him pause before looking into his black eyes. "I want this."

He stepped down into the pool, and his eyes drifted

closed as the water enveloped us.

No matter how hot the day had been, the pool was always cool and refreshing at night, and I relished the feel of it against my heated skin.

"Fresh water," he groaned. "From the mountains..."

"How—"

The sacred pool was fed by a sacred spring guarded by the Faceless Maiden's devotees who watched over the goddess' mountain temple.

But that was a closely guarded secret... men had died for that knowledge.

"I can feel it in the water," he murmured as he opened his black eyes to look at me. "Your secrets are safe with me."

"Why did you come here," I asked.

I was breaking rules—I shouldn't be asking about a worshiper's reason for approaching the temple. I should accept them... no matter the reason.

His smile was faint as he pushed me back toward the edge of the pool. My shoulders struck the mossy stones, and I floated there gently.

"I've been dreaming of you," he murmured as he slid his hands down over my breasts and floated between my legs.

"This is not a dream," I said.

"I know."

He leaned forward to kiss me, and I opened my mouth under his, but the pressure of his lips on mine was all too brief before he pulled away to kiss my jaw and drag his mouth down my throat.

His head disappeared under the surface of the water, and his long white hair spread out around him as he sucked one of my nipples into his mouth.

I moaned and tangled my hand in his hair, conscious of

the fact that he would not be there for long.

But as his fingers, tongue, and teeth teased my nipples to hardness, I lost count of how long he had been underwater.

I was about to pull him to the surface when my thighs were pushed wider apart, and nimble fingers swept over my clit.

"Oh— Goddess," I moaned.

His tongue teased my nipple as his fingers swept over my clit again, and my back arched involuntarily. His mouth dragged down toward my abdomen, and my knees fell open, almost of their own accord.

This time I gripped his hair and reached forward to try to steady myself. My breasts bobbed on the surface of the water as he wrapped his arm around my thigh, and I was certain that my legs were being held open by the weight of the water, and the press of his body against me.

Two fingers slid inside my pussy, and I cried out in surprised ecstasy as his tongue slid between my slick folds.

I wanted to tell him how amazing his tongue felt, how I hoped it would never stop. But he was under the surface of the water... for far too long. And he didn't seem to notice.

He didn't seem to be aware of anything but my pussy.

His fingers thrust deeper as his tongue worked my clit in measured circles before his lips wrapped around my clit and he sucked gently on my swollen core.

I arched against him as his fingers plunged deep and I whimpered to the star-filled sky, desperate for release.

My thighs fell around his shoulders, and my hands dragged through his hair. The waves of it spread out around him in the water like a halo, and I was certain that I would either die in service to the goddess, or I was on the brink of the most amazing orgasm of my life.

As his fingers thrust deeper and faster, his tongue swept over my clit again and again. My thighs twitched and trembled and I pressed my elbows and shoulders into the mossy stones, my hips rolling against his face.

I squeezed my eyes closed and moaned as his teeth grazed against my clit, and an orgasm tore through me.

My whole body shook, and my thighs twitched as I clung to his hair. He stayed there for a moment, riding my orgasm, keeping up the steady rhythm of his fingers and tongue until I was a shivering wreck upon the edge of the pool.

As my climax ebbed away, he pulled his fingers gently from my aching pussy and rose up my body, pausing just long enough to tease my nipples with his mouth before his head broke the surface of the water.

"How—"

He kissed me, hard and hot, and my mouth opened under his. I moaned as his cock pressed against my entrance, but then he pulled away.

"I must tell you something," he murmured.

"Anything—"

I wanted him.

I wanted him more than anything. The goddess' will *must* be satisfied... and mine along with it.

He pushed his wet hair out of his face and looked into my eyes. Captivating me with the darkness of his gaze. "I'm not—what I seem."

I frowned. "What does that mean."

"I am not— This is not how I would present myself to you. To the goddess."

"You are welcome here," I said. "Whoever, and whatever you are. The goddess holds no judgment, and neither do I."

"Do you mean that?" his voice was choked.

I laid a hand upon his cheek. "I do."

He smiled, and then his head fell back. His eyes closed and his lips moved soundlessly.

There was a shift in the water and I reached for him, startled by the change I'd felt—but where my fingers should have touched the hard muscle and bone of his hips, there was smooth, slick flesh in its place.

The strangeness of it made me gasp in surprise and I looked up into his face.

"What—"

"I told you that I came from the eastern shores... and I do. But far to the east. In the midst of the dark waves. The Storm Salts..."

"But—"

These words meant nothing to me.

"This is my true form," he said as he took hold of my wrist. He pulled it through the water toward him.

My breath caught as I felt the way the strangely smooth flesh, slick to the touch, met the hard, lean muscles of his torso.

"How— How are you able—"

"We are all able to walk upon the land, but we prefer the water. Sea water is best, but fresh water is tolerable when it is as clean and blessed as this," he said with a smile.

"What— what are you?"

I worried immediately that I had insulted him, but his smile told me otherwise.

"Morwenna," he said. "That is what my mother called us." His black eyes searched mine as he pushed away from me. A tail that was more fish than anything else rose to the surface, silvered and pale in the moonlight dappled water.

A creature unlike anything I'd ever seen.

A monster. That was what they would call him.

"Are you afraid?"

The goddess' approval thundered through my veins and I lifted my chin.

"No."

The tail disappeared below the surface as he came toward me. His hands gripped my waist, firm and strong, and I wrapped my arms around his neck as he lifted me and guided my legs around his hips.

"Will your goddess bless someone like me?" His voice was choked and I drew him toward me and kissed him hard.

"Without a doubt," I hissed.

I reached between us, and gasped as I encircled his cock with my hand. But the moment I touched it, my eyes widened. The shape of it was different, long and tapered, thicker at the base, and it thrummed with a strange vibration as I touched it. His cock was lubricated with a slick substance that helped my hand to slide along its muscular length without resistance.

But I wasn't one to shy away from the goddess' commands, and her need vibrated through my body, inflaming my own lust and desire to do her will.

I moaned as I guided it toward my entrance. The pulse of his desire flooded my senses as the tip of his cock entered me and the gentle vibration of it trembled against my slick folds.

"Tell me I am not repulsive to you," he murmured.

I smiled and kissed him again and thrust my tongue between his lips as I lifted my hips and impaled myself upon him.

"You are perfection," I moaned.

My eyes shut as he filled me, sliding into me until he was buried to the hilt.

He was warm and smooth, and each time he retreated there was the trace of movement against my clit, teasing me as he thrust into me again. The vibration of his cock was stronger now, and I moaned as I clung to his shoulders. He held my hips as he withdrew, and I braced my feet upon his powerful tail as he flexed and thrust his cock deep into me.

I clung to him as he picked up the pace, and I tightened my arms around his neck as he buried his face in my shoulder. The sound of the water lapping against the rock, the moans and sighs of our pleasure, and the heat that was already building inside of me— it was all I could do not to scream.

My hips bucked against him, and I arched my back to push my breasts into his face. He sucked and nipped at my breasts with teeth that felt sharp and I gasped aloud as he thrust into me, harder and deeper.

The taper of his cock drove me wild with lust and desire and I craved the fullness of the base of his cock, thick and hard inside me.

A sharp twist deep in my belly made me groan and I slid a hand between us to rub my clit. The slickness that lubricated his cock only hastened the speed of my fingers, and my orgasm rushed upon me with a force that made me cry out.

"Come for me, Priestess. Come *with* me." His voice was low and guttural, and I felt the buildup of pressure beginning at my base, the hot coil winding inside of me.

His head dropped forward, his mouth finding my nipple as his hands slid up my back and into my hair.

He pulled my head back as his tongue traced over my throat. "I will bite you. I will spill my seed inside you."

I moaned and arched my neck and my eyes closed as he spoke.

His teeth grazed my neck and his thrusts became short and fast. He buried his face in my neck as he bit me.

My body exploded with the overwhelming pleasure of my orgasm as I felt the sharp hiss of pain. The sensation of his teeth, his hungry mouth on my throat— the feeling of his cock inside me, buried deep— they overwhelmed me and everything lost meaning but the way he possessed me.

His cock swelled inside of me, painfully tight, and I cried out as his seed erupted inside of me. His arms tightened around me, holding me close as the waves of sensation rolled through me.

My climax heightened his pleasure, and I felt his teeth release me as he pressed his face into my shoulder.

"Goddess—"

I moaned and trembled as the goddess' blessings shimmered through my body and my orgasm swelled and swept me away again.

As he pulled away from me, I fell back against the rocks and gasped for breath. My whole body was shuddering, the ripples of my climax still coursing through me.

He floated in front of me, his tail moving gently in the water, and I looked up into his face. All angles and shadows. A pearlescent sheen glowed on the smooth skin of his shoulders and upper chest.

He was beautiful.

A trickle of blood itched its way down my throat and he reached out to wipe it away. I noticed then the webbing between his fingers.

"I did not fully mean to... take your blood, but I did not want to think about the repercussions."

I swallowed and tried to clear my mind. The Goddess'

blessings pounded through my veins in time with my heart and I smiled at him.

"There are no repercussions here," I said as his palm pressed against the side of my neck where it met my shoulder. The pain of the bite had faded away, and all that was left was pleasure that radiated through me in gentle waves.

I laid my hand upon his and did not look away from his deep black gaze. The water lapped gently at my collarbones and I moved toward him.

"I am sorry. I should not have—"

"No," I said as I wound my arms around his neck and floated closer to him so that my breasts brushed against his chest. "It was... it was perfect."

He smiled, and his fingers brushed my cheek, trailing down my neck. "This will heal quickly, but you should clean the wound—"

I took hold of his hand and brought it to my lips. "I'll be fine. When the sun rises, my sisters will return and they will care for me. Any injuries will be healed by their expert hands and the goddess' grace."

"Dawn—"

He glanced at the trees, and his black eyes widened as he saw the edge of the red dawn moon.

"I must go."

He pressed his lips to mine in a lingering kiss, and then he pulled away and sank down into the depths of the pool. His white hair spread out around him as it lapped over his head, and I waited for him to resurface.

Strong, slender hands gripped my waist as he rose up in the water and I smiled as he broke the surface and pushed the wet hair out of his face. He pressed his long body against mine, and I gasped against his mouth to feel his very real cock—the same one that I'd taken into my mouth before we'd entered the pool—press against my thigh.

"Can I see you again," he murmured.

I shook my head. "No," I said. "It is forbidden."

Disappointment was evident in his expression. "Will you remember me?"

"Every night," I whispered and kissed him gently.

With a strangled groan he pulled himself away from me and climbed out of the pool.

I rested my forearms against the mossy stones and watched him dry himself with his tunic before he pulled his breeches up over his lithe legs and fastened his belt around his hips.

"I wish you well," I said. "Go with the goddess' blessing. And mine."

I bit down hard on my tongue as soon as the words left my mouth, I knew I had made a mistake.

I was not here to speak for myself... I was here to speak for the goddess and be her vessel.

His smile made my pussy tighten and I dug my fingernails into the moss-covered rocks. It would be so easy to leave—to disappear into the woods with my lover.

To forsake my place in the goddess' service...

No.

I could never leave this place.

I was born here. I belonged to the Faceless Maiden. There was nothing else for me.

"Be safe," he said as he turned toward the woods. "Perhaps I will see you again."

I did not answer him, not aloud.

Perhaps.

I bit down hard on my lip as I replayed my moments of worship with the morwenna who had come to the temple... I had never met anyone like him, and it was possible that I never would again.

I rubbed my fingers over the rune that had etched its way onto my skin, covering the bite wound he had made on my shoulder. Every time I saw it or rubbed my fingers over the small scars he had left behind, I remembered him.

I slid two fingers into my pussy, and then three, but it wasn't enough.

My other hand teased my clit with more urgency, tight circles that would bring me to climax.

"Are we interrupting you, Priestess?" a voice called out.

Startled, I pulled my fingers from my pussy and swam to the edge of the pool.

My pulse pounded in my throat as I rose up to peer into the darkness.

"Whoever you are," I called back. "You are welcome to this temple. Have you come to seek the favor of the Faceless Maiden? If you have, you must leave your weapons at the edge of the trees—approach these sacred stones with love."

A hooded figure emerged from the shadows and approached. I could sense her hesitation, and wondered if she had ever been among the sanctuary trees before. "We—"

Her voice dropped to a whisper.

"We seek the favor of the Faceless Maiden," she said slowly. Her words were accented, lilting and melodic.

"We? Where is your companion?"

"He waits in the trees," she said.

My pussy tightened when I noticed that she was alone. I

was still wet from my own touch and I pressed my thighs together and relished the thrill that shuddered up my spine.

She was beautiful, with long dark hair that floated around the hooded cloak that covered her and brushed over the grass.

I could see nothing of her body, but I wondered if she had come here naked...

The thought of being seen by this woman—of being watched while I pleasured myself—made me burn with expectation.

"Come," I said as I pushed myself up out of the pool. The moss was soft under my feet and I relished the way the woman's eyes widened. "Let me look at you."

A small smile tugged at the woman's lips as I approached her. She stood still as I pushed back the hood of her cloak and traced my fingers along the length of the pin that held her cloak at her shoulder. The red-brown metal was marked out with rich green stains, but it was like nothing I'd ever seen.

"What is this metal?" I asked.

"Narthyx," she replied. "Mined from the Southlands. My homeland."

She pushed her dark hair behind her ears to show me their roundness. It had been an age since a human had walked into the goddess' sacred glade.

"If you have come here to seek her favor, I welcome you to her temple," I said. But the goddess' response was low in my consciousness—a low thrum. I needed more. "The goddess wishes for your companion to join us," I said.

I traced my fingers over the roundness of her ear and down her jaw to rub my thumb over her lower lip.

"He is nervous," she said. "He is not accustomed to the kindness of the goddess."

"Then let us make him more accustomed," I said with a smile.

She reached up to pull the pin from the fine wool of her cloak. It fell to the ground and my breath caught as I drank in the sight of her naked body.

Her nipples were small and dark, hardening in the chill of the evening breeze and I smiled as I brushed my fingers down her throat and over her collarbones.

"Perhaps we might coax him from the shadows," I said.

She smiled and took hold of my other hand as she stepped closer to me. Her lips pressed against mine, warm and eager, and my mouth opened for her kiss.

She was smaller than I, shorter with small, high breasts and a trim waist that curved down to generous hips and a triangle of dark hair nestled between the softness of her thighs.

Her kiss was hungry, and she moaned as her breasts flattened against mine. Her other hand wrapped around my waist to pull me against her and my breath caught as she gripped my ass.

As her lips left mine and she pressed her mouth against my throat, my head fell back, I was conscious of the fact that another set of eyes watched us from the forest, and a thrill ran through my body as the goddess' approval for this union began to grow.

The dark-haired woman released her grip on my hand and reached up to take hold of my breast. She bent her head and sucked my nipple into her mouth, and I wrapped my arms around her to hold her there and encourage her attentions.

I could feel the hooded woman's heat against my thigh and I reached down to place my fingers between her legs. I stroked her gently, exploring her secret folds with gentle motions as she moaned against my breasts.

She was wet, her entrance smooth as I stroked her and my hunger grew as I imagined this woman writhing beneath me as my tongue tormented her clit.

Her hips bucked forward, encouraging my explorations, and I slid one finger inside her. She was still for a moment, the warmth of her breath against my breasts as she sucked on my nipple. Then she moaned and thrust forward, taking more of my finger, craving more.

She rocked against my fingers, and I responded by sliding my other hand down her back to cup her round ass. Her hips moved faster, matching the speed of my fingers, and her moans grew deeper, her lips parting to allow the sound to escape.

I leaned forward and placed a kiss on the woman's shoulder, then pulled my fingers from her slit and pushed them into her wet mouth, forcing her to taste her own arousal.

She moaned as she sucked on my fingers, and I looked back at the dark outline of the forest.

Where was her companion?

"Come out, my friend," I called out.

"The goddess grows impatient."

I looked back at the woman, who smiled at me and eased forward to kiss me once more. I tasted her slick arousal as her tongue rubbed against mine. Her hands wandered over my body, mapping out the curves and slopes of my skin and she squeezed my ass and pulled me closer to her.

I could feel the length of her body against mine and my

heart raced as I wondered what her lover would be like. Her body was warm and welcoming, and her skin felt like satin beneath my fingers. She pulled away from me and took my hand to pull me down onto the moss beside the pool.

I lay down on my side and she pressed her body against mine. I could feel her tight curves against my waist, and I wanted to revel in her body, but the thirst for her lover's touch drove me forward.

I felt his presence long before he stepped into the torchlight.

His eyes were a deep brown, and the hair that hung in loose curls around his face was dark, almost black.

I could see the tension in his body, the nervousness in the way he held his shoulders and the tremor that ran through his hands. He was tall and muscular, but his jaw was covered in scruff and I smiled as I imagined kissing him as I'd kissed the woman beside me.

The black tattoos of the Faceless Goddess covered his chest and ran down his arms.

His cock pressed against his leather breeches and my mouth went dry as I looked up at him.

"I've dreamed of you," he said, "dreamed of returning to the Goddess' sanctuary—"

I pushed up on my elbow, panic overtaking the desire that had so recently consumed me. "You are a servant of the Maiden—"

"I—"

His voice was choked and as I gazed at him, taking in the intricate runes that were etched across his skin, the goddess' approval thundered through me.

She had accepted him. And so must I.

"You are welcome here," I said with a smile. My hand

trailed over the curve of the dark-haired woman's waist. "Will you come and worship with us?"

He nodded and untied the lacing that held his breeches at his hips. He pushed them down and stepped free of them and the woman beside me smiled as he approached us, naked and erect.

I smiled as I watched him, taking in the taper of his waist, the lean muscles of his thighs, and the way the marks of the Goddess snaked around his calves.

He had been blessed but Her favor. But I did not recognize him.

"Where have you come from," I asked.

"Does it matter?" the woman asked me.

It didn't matter.

The woman beside me rose up to kneel in front of him, and with a whispered word of encouragement, she gently took hold of his cock and eased him forward.

He moaned as she sucked on his cock, and he reached out to grasp her head and threaded his fingers through her dark hair as she took him deep into her throat. He held her there for a moment, three heartbeats, and then he released her, and she drew back. Breathing hard, she looked up at him with an eager smile upon her beautiful face.

His fingers tightened in her dark tresses as he guided his cock back into her mouth, and I rolled onto my knees to join them. He glanced at me, his eyes wide, and I smiled.

His hand caressed my cheek as I laid a hand against his thigh, my other on the small of her back. He turned to the woman who knelt between his legs. She opened her mouth, inviting him to enter, and he pressed forward.

His cock slid between her lips, and she moaned as he slid deeper. Then he released her hair, and cupped her face in his hands as he thrust forward. Faster and faster his hips pumped, driving his cock into her mouth and throat, and her moans echoed around us as she struggled to keep pace with him. One of her arms wrapped around my waist, the other around his thigh as he used her, urging him on with her moans.

My hand slipped down her ass and teased at her soaking entrance from behind as she took his cock in her mouth.

She whimpered and moaned, pushing back against me, and I slipped two fingers inside her.

The man relaxed his hold on her face, pulled his cock from her mouth. I thrust my fingers into her soaking pussy, trying to mimic the rhythm of the cock that had just ravaged her throat.

His cock glistened with her saliva, and I smiled as he turned back to me. I leaned forward eagerly to take his cockhead in my mouth as his companion rode my hand with vigor.

He groaned as I tasted his cock, and I sucked him deep into my throat. The woman beneath me moaned loudly as my fingers thrust up into her, matching the speed of my tongue as it slid up and down the man's shaft.

I looked up at him, eager to see his expression, but my eyes were drawn to the woman's glistening buttocks. I drew back from his cock and ran my tongue up his shaft, the length of his cock, and then scooted forward.

She moaned out her pleasure as I wrapped my fingers around her hip, holding her in place as I buried my face between her ass cheeks and licked at her tight hole while my fingers plunged into her pussy.

"Yes," she moaned, and thrust back against my face. "Yes, Goddess."

Her juices flowed freely, coating my lips and chin as I licked at her and thrust my tongue into her entrance to fill her as completely as I could.

I wanted her. The goddess wanted her.

In front of us, the man smiled.

"Take her—I can feel the goddess' desire for her."

I pulled back from her and she looked over her shoulder at me in surprise.

"Turn over," I commanded.

She responded in an instant and rolled over onto her back. Her moan was breathless as her thighs parted for me.

I knelt between her legs and ran my hands up the length of her thighs, feeling the tension in them. My fingers trailed over the curve of her hip and I leaned forward to kiss her as I knelt between her thighs.

"Please," she whispered, and I smiled.

I slid up her body, kissing her just below her navel, feeling her shiver beneath my lips. I reached up and cupped her breasts, and she arched her back with a soft moan as I rolled her nipples between my fingers.

"Please," she whispered again and she reached down for me and pulled me up to kiss me.

I could taste the musk of her partner's cock on her lips as they opened under mine, and I felt the tension tighten in her body, the grip of her desire tighten in my arms.

I kissed her hard and fast, and then lowered my head to kiss her neck, and then my lips trailed down her chest. I nipped at her breasts as I pulled her nipples between my teeth.

"Oh yes," she breathed, "take me, Goddess."

I reached down between us legs and slid two fingers into her wetness. She gasped as they filled her, and her hips thrust up toward me. I withdrew my fingers and pressed my lips to hers, sliding my tongue into her mouth as my fingers entered her again.

She moaned against my kiss and I pulled away to busy my head against her breasts as I thrust my fingers into her again.

"Yes," she cried out, "please!"

I pressed my fingers into her once more, and suckled on her nipple as my other hand found her clit and I circled it with my thumb.

Her moans sounded like a prayer, and as I licked up the valley between her breasts, I could feel her muscles tighten and her need build.

The Goddess' approval thrummed through me in a powerful rush, and I knew that she yearned for the woman as I did.

The dark haired woman shuddered beneath me and I drove my fingers into her again as I dragged myself down her body.

Her hands gripped my hair and she writhed beneath me, lifting her hips up to me, begging me to take her, and I smiled against her stomach.

"Yes," she moaned as I slid my fingers from her. "Goddess, please!"

I settled between her legs, my hair brushing against her thighs and I kissed the smooth skin of her thigh as I inhaled her sweetly musky scent. I stroked my hand up her leg, feeling her muscles relax with the soft touch.

I slid my fingers into her eager entrance again, as she moaned and thrust her hips up toward me, begging for more. I leaned down to press my lips against her and she cried out, her body shuddering beneath me as my fingers slid into her, filling her to the hilt.

She moaned as I lowered my face to her pussy, and I licked my way up the length of her. Her thighs trembled against my shoulders as I slid my tongue into her entrance and thrust my fingers into her again and again.

"Please, Goddess," she moaned softly as my tongue slid up to her clit and I pressed it between my lips.

Her hips bucked up against me as I licked and sucked at her clit, tormenting her until she writhed from the ecstasy of my attentions.

I had almost forgotten about her companion, but I was reminded of his presence as his fingertips skimmed over my hip and down the curve of my ass.

"She is almost ready," he whispered in my ear and I moaned against the woman's pussy. "Are *you* ready?"

The dark-haired woman writhed beneath me. She was close to her climax, and the goddess' lust thundered through me.

I tongued her clit harder as I thrust my fingers deep inside her, and with a gasp her hand tightened in my hair and she cried out as her climax crashed over her.

The man moved behind us and placed his hand on the small of my back.

With my face still buried in his companion's sweet pussy, intent on lapping up all of her juices, I arched back against his hand and then moaned as his cock slid between my ass cheeks and then pressed against my wet pussy.

The dark haired woman released her hold on my hair and pulled me toward her. I lifted my face from her pussy and crawled up her body. She rose up to kiss me hungrily as the thick head of her partner's cock nudged at my entrance.

Her mouth pressed against mine as the man behind me moved quickly, filling me with his cock in one smooth thrust.

The woman's kiss was frantic, and her hands gripped my hair as he thrust into me again.

He groaned above me as his cock slid into me and my pussy clenched around his hot length.

He pressed my down against the woman beneath me as he fucked me. Sensation washed over me in waves, and the Goddess' approval thrummed through me.

The man's cock twitched and swelled inside me, and I moaned into the woman's mouth as she slid her fingers into my hair.

His groans filled my ears, and he thrust into me again, harder and faster, his cock jerking and throbbing inside me.

"Yes," I moaned as I looked into the woman's eyes and my pussy clenched around his cock.

His hand grasped the back of my neck and I arched my back against the cock that slid against my pussy. His hand was rough on my neck, his fingers callused.

The woman smiled up at me as her hand snaked between us, and I moaned aloud as she began to tease her fingers against my clit. I was slick with arousal, and she moaned as she circled her companion's cock with her fingers.

"That's right," he groaned. "Feel me fucking her."

The woman licked at my breasts, teasing my nipples with her teeth as she pushed her fingers into my aching pussy to augment her companion's thrusts.

My body thrummed with arousal, and my muscles tightened around the man's cock as my climax closed in.

"The captive of the goddess," he groaned. "You're so fucking beautiful." His cock slammed into me and his words were rough and breathless.

I whimpered as the woman slid her fingers from between my thighs. My body ached for her touch, the

Goddess' approval thrummed through me. With a cry the man released my neck and gripped my shoulders tightly.

I could feel the rush of his climax and I pushed back against him to meet his thrusts.

"Yes, give it to me," I moaned, "fill me."

He cried out and thrust his cock deep into me.

His guttural groan accompanied the hot spurt of his seed as he filled my pussy.

My own orgasm washed over me in intense waves and my body tightened and shuddered. The dark haired woman held me tight against her, and she murmured sweet encouragement before she kissed me hard as I convulsed and came on his cock.

The Goddess' approval filled me. It throbbed in my blood, and pounded behind my eyes and in my pussy.

He pulled out of me and I moaned as I rocked against the woman beneath me. The Faceless Maiden cried out in my head, and I felt her pleasure as I arched against the dark-haired woman.

The goddess' approval flooded through me as I felt my orgasm building again as the woman rubbed her fingers against my engorged clit.

In my head, the goddess cried out again and our climax was almost simultaneous. Her joy and release flooded through me like a hot rush, and I felt her pleasure as I whimpered and moaned.

I slowed my hips and ground against the woman beneath me.

"So beautiful," she murmured and the man's fingers slid into my hair and he pushed my head down so that my face was buried in the curve of her neck.

She tasted like dew and flowers, and her skin was soft and sweet under my lips.

The scent of my own arousal filled my nostrils as a deep and satisfied moan escaped my lips.

With slow and languid strokes, the woman continued to make love to me and I melted against her as she coaxed another, gentler, orgasm from my exhausted body.

In my head, the goddess' approval filled me, and I knew that she had enjoyed herself as much as I had. I could feel her sated pleasure. I could feel the tenderness of her caress as the woman stroked my hair.

As I collapsed on top of her, the woman placed a soft kiss upon my lips.

"A worthy vessel," she murmured before she rolled to her side and pulled me with her. She lay with me until my vision blurred, her touch was soft against my face and the soft murmur of her companion's voice was soothing to my ears. I relished his warmth as he stretched out behind me and stroked his callused hands down my side.

Bliss.

It was bliss to be so cherished.

They left me in the soft moss at the edge of the sacred pool, and watched sleepily as the pair washed themselves in the blessed waters, dressed, and then departed without a backward glance.

I had so many questions—where had they come from. To which temple did he belong... and why had the Maiden accepted him if he had left the order?

But as I lay on the soft ground and inhaled the scent of the grass and the approaching dawn, none of it mattered.

I would have to tell the High Priestess what had happened, as I did on every night of my service... but all that mattered was that I had done the bidding of the goddess and carried out her will.

That was my purpose here.

I gasped as the familiar burn of the goddess' runes as they etched themselves onto my skin.

Two worshippers. United as one.

Two unique runes traced over my flesh.

Etched in a joined pair above my right hip, I would remember them forever... just as I remembered all of the others.

Another delicious night in the service of the Faceless Maiden.

I dragged myself to the edge of the sacred pool and sighed as I rolled into the water. I relished the chill of it against my heated skin and leaned against the edge of the pool to catch my breath and wait for the throb of the goddess' release to ebb away.

When the sun rose, my sister priestesses would flood into the temple and I would be relieved of my duties. I would be taken into the sacred precinct to share my exploits with the High Priestess and tell them who had entered our grove—and what they had demanded of me.

I would be seen by healers if I needed them, and given the comfort of a massage and the care of the sisters...

I loved my position here.

I had been chosen... and there was nothing that would change that. Not now. Not ever.

I had been marked with the goddess' favor, and even if those marks were burned from my flesh, *I* would still remember.

KRATERRAN KINGDOMS

ORC WARLORD

Orc's Unwilling Bride

Orc's Captive Bride

Orc's Vengeful Bride

***

ORC REBEL

Betrayed by the Orc

Claimed by the Orc

Rescued by the Orc

***

ORC BROTHERHOOD

Protected by the Orc

***

FAE SURROGATES

Seducing the Fae King

Betrayed by the Fae King

Stolen by the Fae King

Owned by the Fae King

***

STANDALONE NOVELS

Wild Heart

Kraterran Kingdoms

9 798215 534724

Printed by Libri Plureos GmbH in Hamburg,
Germany